MW00876007

**Barrington Area Library**

505 North Northwest Highway
Barrington, Illinois 60010
847/382-1300

DEMCO

A PICTURE READER

# OTTO the CAT

By Gail Herman
Illustrated by Norman Gorbaty

Grosset & Dunlap • New York

Otto is a  .

He lives in a  .

"My  ," says Otto.

He has a .

"My ," says Otto.

Otto even has a  .

Today Otto wants to go

to the pet store.

What does Otto want?

He wants a new  .

He wants

a new toy 🐭 .

Otto gets everything

he wants.

Does he want a  ?

No!

Too late!

The  wants Otto.

He wags his  .

"Out of my  !"

says Otto.

The stays put.

"Out of my  !"

says Otto.

The  stays put.

"Out of my 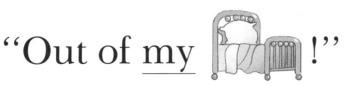 !"

Otto tells the  .

"Do not play with

my toy  .

Do not eat from

my blue  ."

What can Otto do?

Everywhere he goes,

the  goes too.

All at once,

Otto knows what to do.

He runs out of the

to the .

The runs too!

I will run

around and around.

I will make the

 dizzy.

Then I will run back.

And he will not find

my .

Otto runs around.

At last, he stops.

Otto is dizzy.

But is the  dizzy?

No!

The  is not

dizzy at all.

He picks Otto up.

He takes him to

the  .

"My  ," says Otto.

"My 🚗 .

My blue 🥣 .

My toy 🐭 .

My 🛏 ."

Otto looks at the .

"<u>My</u> ," says Otto.